To Vic and Leo

British Library Cataloguing in publication Data available

ISBN 0 216 92180 5

Blackie and Son Ltd
7 Leicester Place
London WC2H 7BP

First American edition published in 1988 by
Peter Bedrick Books
125 East 23rd Street
New York NY 10010

Library of Congress Cataloging-in-Publication Data

Eaton, Su.
Hey presto!

Summary: After Mr. Thomas the magician performs at her birthday
party, Vicky asks him to magically fix a little bird's broken wing.
[1. Magicians — Fiction] I. Bridle, Martin.
II. Title.
PZ7.E145He 1988 [E] 87-33375

ISBN 0-87226-182-4

Filmset by Deltatype, Ellesmere Port
Printed in Great Britain by Cambus Litho

HEY PRESTO!

Su Eaton and Martin Bridle

**BLACKIE
LONDON**

**BEDRICK/BLACKIE
NEW YORK**

Mr Thomas lives at Number 24 Warlock Way.

Vicky lives at Number 22.

Mr Thomas has a secret. On certain days he becomes
a conjuror – a magic man! And this is one of those special days.

Today is Vicky's birthday – but that's no secret!
She has sent party invitations to all her friends.

Vicky waits for her friends to comc. When everyone
has arrived, the party can begin.

They don't know that Mr Thomas is coming too.
He's an unexpected guest.

When the games are over it is time for tea. Vicky blows
out the candles on her cake and makes a wish.

After tea it is time for the magic show.
Vicky's wish has come true!

Mr Thomas is very clever.
'It's impossible!'

Mr Thomas is very funny.
'It's hilarious!'

Mr Thomas asks Vicky to help him with the magic.
'HEY PRESTO!'

When the show is finished, it is time to go home.
'Thank you for coming, Mr Thomas.'

When the birthday is over, it's time to go to bed,

and when it's time
to go to bed,
it's time to dream.

In the morning the dreams are over and it is time
to get up. It is a new day and anything seems possible.

'Ladies and gentlemen, I'm Vicky,
the wonderful conjuror!'

While she is playing in the garden, Vicky finds a bird
with a broken wing. She wonders if her spell will make it better.

'HEY PRESTO!' But the magic doesn't work.

Vicky asks Mr Thomas to help.
Perhaps he knows some
special secret words.

'This needs a different kind of magic,' whispers Mr Thomas.
'We must keep the wing in the right position
with some sticky tape. Gently does it!'

'With a bit of skill,
some love, and plenty of time,
we might be lucky.'

Every day they feed the bird
and watch it grow stronger.

At last the wing is mended and it is time
to let the little bird go. 'HEY PRESTO!'

'Which was the real magic, magic man?'